Apollo's Chariot

希臘羅馬神話故事 ❿

阿波羅戰車 Apollo's Chariot

First Published May, 2011
First Printing May, 2011

Original Story by Thomas Bulfinch
Rewritten by Brian Stuart
Illustrated by Penelope Gamble
Designer by Eonju No
Translated by Jia-chen Chuo

Printed and distributed by Cosmos Culture Ltd.
Tel: 02-2365-9739
Fax: 02-2365-9835
http://www.icosmos.com.tw
Publisher: Value-Deliver Culture Ltd.

Copyright © Happy House 2003
First published by Happy House, Seoul, Korea

Taiwanese Edition Copyright © Value-Deliver Culture Ltd. 2011
Taiwanese edition is published by arrangement with Happy House.

Welcome to the World of Mythology

Mythology gives interesting explanations about many tribulations in life and tries to satisfy your curiosity. Many stories have been created to explain surprising or frightening phenomena. Thus, different countries and peoples throughout the world have their own myths.

Greek and Roman mythology is deeply loved, because it is a treasury of imagination that weaves together the exciting legends of surreal gods, heroines, and heroes. As a mirror that reflects the human world, Greek and Roman mythology is recommended as a must-read in order to understand western culture and thinking.

Although the basis of these classical stories can be traced back as far as the prehistoric age, what is it in these myths that can still enchant you, a citizen of the contemporary world? The secret is that mythology transcends time and space and keeps intact the internal desires of human beings. The exciting adventures allow you unlimited access to the important aspects of life: war and peace, life and death, good and evil, and love and hatred.

The Olympian gods who appear in Greek and Roman mythology are not always described as perfect, omnipotent gods. As these gods fight in anger, trick other gods, and suffer the pain of love and jealousy, they often resemble humans. In Let's Enjoy Mythology, the second volume in the series Reading Greek and Roman Mythology in English, you can encounter many heroes, heroines, gods, and goddesses with very human characteristics.

Reading Greek and Roman Mythology in English will guide you through your journey into the imaginary world of the ancient Greeks. Your trip will be to a place that transcends time and space.

The characters in the stories

Phaeton
He was the son of the god of the sun, Apollo, and the nymph Clymene. To prove that he was the son of Apollo, Phaeton drove Apollo's chariot, was hit by Zeus's lightening bolt, and died.

Apollo
He was the son of Zeus. Apollo was the god of the sun, prophecy, medicine, archery, and music. As the most handsome god, he was the twin brother of Artemis, the goddess of the moon and hunt. Clymene, a nymph, bore him a son, Phaeton.

Clymene
She was a nymph and the daughter of Oceanus, the god of the water, and Tethys, one of the twelve Titans. Clymene had seven daughters and a son with the god of the sun, Apollo. Phaeton was one of these sons.

Zeus
He was the king of the gods and the strongest of all the gods. Zeus was accorded supreme authority on Mount Olympus and on earth. He used thunderbolts as weapons that could destroy anything.

Poseidon
He was the brother of Zeus and the god of the sea and water. Poseidon had a trident, with which he could command the clouds, rain, winds, and waves. When Zeus was waging the war against the Titans, Poseidon fought bravely with Zeus. And in the Trojan War, he protected the Greek forces.

Demeter
She was the goddess of the crops and harvest and was Zeus's sister. Demeter searched all over the world for her daughter who was abducted by the god of the Underworld, Hades. Demeter was recognized in many regions and was worshipped all across Greece.

Phaeton was the son of the god of the sun, Apollo, and the nymph Clymene. He was very proud of the fact that his father was Apollo. However, friends of Phaeton would not believe him. They laughed at him, asking him to show proof that he was Apollo's son. Finally, he set out to find Apollo and demonstrate their relationship to the world. Then, for the first time after his birth, he met his father.

Apollo promised to grant Phaeton anything that he might want. This would be proof that Phaeton was his son. In response, Phaeton made a big wish. He declared that he would like to drive the sun chariot, which no one but Apollo could drive. However, driving the chariot was so dangerous that even Zeus, the king of the gods, was reluctant to drive it. Apollo had no choice but to grant Phaeton's wish, because he had already sworn an oath before the Styx River.

Despite Apollo's effort to persuade and beg him not to drive the chariot, Phaeton set off driving the chariot, and finally he found himself in big trouble. As Apollo had warned, Phaeton couldn't control the horses, and they broke loose from their course across the sky. This brought catastrophe upon heaven where the gods resided and the earth where humans lived. Does the fall of Phaeton still affect those of us living in the contemporary world? Can you imagine what happened?

Contents

1

PHAETON, THE SON OF APOLLO

"If you are really the son of Apollo,
prove it!"

I n ancient Ethiopia,
there lived a boy named Phaeton.
His mother was a nymph, Clymene,
and his father was the sun god, Apollo.

One day Phaeton was playing
with his friends.
He boasted, "My father is the sun god."
But Phaeton's friends laughed.
They teased Phaeton by saying,
"Your father really isn't the Sun.
Your mother just made
that up because your
real father wouldn't
marry her.
You are foolish to
believe such a story.
If you are really
the son of Apollo,
prove it!"

But Phaeton had no proof.
He went home confused and ashamed.

As soon as he got home,
he went to his mother.
"Mom, am I really the child of the Sun?
No one believes me."
Clymene sighed and said,
"My son, if I lie, let the sun kill me instantly.
Your father truly is the Sun that gives us
warmth and light."

"But I can only give you my word as proof.
If you do not believe me, why don't you go
and ask your father, Apollo?
His palace is in the mountains on the
eastern edge of the land."
Phaeton was overjoyed to hear his mother's
simple plan.

That night, he prepared a bag for his
journey and slept soundly.

The next morning, he said goodbye to his mother and started walking towards the rising sun.

His journey took him through India.

He saw many wonders there.

Sometimes, he wanted to stop and explore the cities and also talk to the people.

But he had a goal.

Every day, he got closer to his father.
So Phaeton did not stop except to eat
and sleep.

It took him just a
week to arrive at
the mountains on
the eastern edge of
the land.
He climbed into
the mountains
and fell asleep.

2

THE SUN GOD, APOLLO

Apollo smiled gently and hugged his son tightly.

T he next morning, long before dawn, he woke up. He saw a strange light. Phaeton climbed up a steep hill and saw a palace. Immediately he knew it was the palace of the sun god, Apollo.

The palace was made of gold and bronze.
What an amazing place!
Tall white marble columns supported the entire building.
A white staircase led up to the doors.
There were two huge shining silver doors at the entrance.

Phaeton started to climb the stairs.

As he got near the top, he could see pictures carved on the palace walls.

Hephaestus, the master craftsman of the gods, had made this palace.

He carved pictures of the earth, sea, and heavens on the walls.

When Phaeton got to the top,
the huge silver doors opened.
He went inside the palace and
entered a huge room.
Phaeton stopped at a distance,
because the light was so bright that
he couldn't see well.

It was the hall of the sun god, Apollo.
Before him there was an amazing sight.
Upon a throne at the far end
sat the sun god.
He wore a purple robe.
On his head was a crown that shone
with the light of the sun.
It seemed to be made of pure, white light.
Apollo's throne glittered
because of the many diamonds
on its sides.

The bright light hurt Phaeton's eyes.
So Phaeton first looked at the gods and
goddesses on both sides of the throne.
On Apollo's right stood the Year, Month,
and Day.
On his left stood the gods and goddesses of
the four seasons.

Spring was a yellow-haired young woman in
a bright green robe.
Flowers seemed to grow down out of her hair.
They covered her body.

Beside her was Summer.
She was a slightly older, dark-haired woman.
She had a crown made of grain.

Next to Summer
stood Autumn,
a middle-aged man.
His hair was brown and gray.
His robe was made of orange,
yellow, and red leaves.
His bare feet were stained
with grape juice.
He had a bunch of grapes in
his hands.

Last of all was Winter,
an old man.
His white hair and beard
seemed blue with frost.
They were stiff
like icicles.

At first sight, Apollo recognized his son.
The sun god's eyes blazed like fire as he spoke.
"Why have you come here to the far edge of
the earth, Phaeton?"
The boy replied,
"Oh, great Apollo, and Father if that is true.
I have come to find proof that you are really
my father."
Apollo smiled gently and hugged his son
tightly.

3

PHAETON'S WISH

"I wish to drive your chariot, father."

He took off the crown that hurt
Phaeton's eyes, and set it aside.
"Your mother has told you the truth.
I am your father. To prove it,
I will give you anything that you ask for.
I swear it by the river Styx, which we gods
swear by in our most solemn promises."
Phaeton immediately replied,
"I wish to drive your chariot, father."
"No, my child, please choose something
else. Anything but that.
Your wish is too dangerous.
Even Zeus, the father of the gods,
will not drive the chariot of the sun."

"The chariot is too hot for you.

The horses themselves breathe fire.

They are very strong.

It is even difficult for me to control them.

I am sorry that I made such a promise to

you. Please, choose something else."

Apollo tried to persuade Phaeton.

But he did not change his mind.

Apollo tried to scare Phaeton.

"I swore by the river Styx,

and I cannot break my promise.

But beware my son, the way through the

heavens is full of danger.

On your way up, the road is steep.

You will go very high.

But do not look down!

You'll become dizzy and fall."

"In the heavens, you will not find the
houses of the gods.
The gods live still higher.
Instead, you must drive by the terrible
monsters that live between the stars.
There is Taurus, the mighty bull.
Beware his horns! Beware also the arrows
from Archer!" said Apollo.

"Your path will also
lead by Leo,
the fierce lion.
He has sharp claws
and teeth.
You must drive
between the claws
of both Crab and Scorpion, too.

At the same time,
you must watch out
for Scorpion's stinger.
It is full of horrible
poison.
If it strikes you,
you will die slowly and
terribly.
All the while,
the heavens are turning around,
so you must pay attention,"said Apollo.

"But even if you pass through the heavens,
you are not safe yet.
The most difficult part is the way down.
It is as steep as the way up.
It requires all my skill not to lose control.
Tethys, the goddess of the ocean,
waits for me on the other side. She is often
afraid that I will come falling down.
You are only a mortal boy.
I fear that my gift will kill you," said Apollo.

Apollo and Chariot

Phaeton listened, but he was not afraid.

He wanted to show the world that he was really Apollo's son.

The time for sunrise was getting near.

Apollo sighed and took his son to the huge chariot.

This magical vehicle was the gift of Hephaestus.

It was made of solid gold and silver.

The chariot shone brightly with a light of its own.

Along the seat were gems such as rubies, emeralds, and diamonds.

When the lights from Apollo's crown hit them, they sparkled brightly.

Twenty-four young goddesses stood by.

They were the Hours of the day.

Their job was to make the horses ready.

This pair of tall white horses struck the
ground with their huge hooves.

Their hooves were coated with special oil.

This oil allowed the horses to fly.

The horses seemed anxious to start their
daily journey.

Phaeton stood near the chariot.

He could feel the heat of the horses' breath.

Suddenly, the darkness of the sky became rosy.

Aurora had opened the curtains of her nearby palace.
She was the goddess of the Dawn.
Every morning the light from her bedroom signaled a new day.
Apollo tried one last time.

"It is time for the chariot to begin its journey.
But there is still time for me to take your place.
Listen to me son, and do not do this."
But Phaeton still wouldn't change his mind.
The horses and the chariot had filled him with pride.
He did not yet fear their terrible power.

Apollo took a jar from one of the Hours. From it, he poured some oil on Phaeton's hair and face.

"My son, this magic oil will protect you from the heat of my crown."

Then the sun god placed the crown of light on Phaeton's head.

This time,
the light did not hurt the boy's eyes.

Apollo gave his son final instructions.

"Do not hit the horses to make them go faster.

They will not slow down by themselves.

Instead, you must hold onto the reins with all your strength."

"Do not let them slip from your hands!
If you lose them, you will lose control of the
chariot. Then there will be great danger for
both the heavens and the earth.
If you go too high,
you will burn the houses of the gods.
If you go too low,
you will kill both humans and animals.
The middle course is the safest and the best.
It will give the earth and the heavens the
proper amount of heat and light.
Follow the wheel marks that I have left

day after day.
These will
help to guide
your way."

One of the
Hours pushed
open the
purple doors
and covered
the pathway
with red
roses.
Far away to
the west,
Apollo could
see his sister,
the Moon.

She was just finishing her journey across
the heavens.
The stars in the sky were being led away
by the morning star.
The sun was supposed to rise as soon as
the morning star disappeared.

4

PHAETON ON THE CHARIOT

He tried to pull the reins,
but the horses ignored him.

Phaeton jumped up into the driver's seat.
One of the Hours offered him the reins.
Phaeton took them.

The horses lifted their heads.

The gate was opened. With a snort of fire
and smoke, the horses moved forward.

Phaeton felt the chariot leap forward.

For a second, he imagined the chariot was alive.

The horses
pushed the
clouds aside.
Their powerful
legs pounded
the road.

Phaeton on the Chariot

At first, Phaeton was excited.
But the horses felt that their load was lighter. The person who held their reins was weaker. So they ran faster and wilder than before.
This caused the chariot to move from side to side. For the first time, Phaeton regretted his choice.

He tried to pull the reins,
but the horses ignored him.
Soon they ran off the road into the
wide-open universe.

The light of the sun rose in the east.

But instead of getting stronger,

the light became weaker!

Higher and higher the horses climbed.

Soon the rays of the sun disappeared!

Dawn turned back into night.

The people of the earth were confused.

The promise of a new day was suddenly gone!

The sun became just another star in the

inky black sky.

The sun god's horses ran toward the North Star. The approach of the chariot warmed the North Pole.

The Serpent that lay around the North Pole felt the heat of the sun for the first time.

It had not moved for a long time because of the cold. But now it woke up from the heat. It hissed. The snake's poisonous breath filled the North Pole.

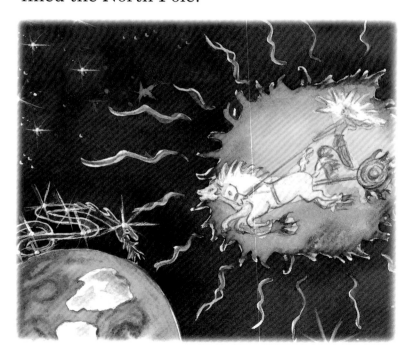

The creatures in heaven also felt the
heat.
The Great Bear and the Little Bear
couldn't stand the heat.
They felt as if they would burn up.
They wanted to jump into the sea,
but they couldn't.

Phaeton looked down and felt sick.

The earth was growing smaller and smaller under him.

His face became pale and his knees shook with terror. He tried to look up.

But it was no relief.

Ahead, he saw a horrible sight. The horses were running straight for Scorpion! The huge monster raised its tail. Phaeton could see the poison dripping from the stinger.

Then he smelled the poison.

It twisted his stomach.

He dropped the reins and held onto the chariot.

The horses felt the reins go loose.

Suddenly, they plunged downwards, toward the earth.

Closer and closer they came.

Phaeton could see rivers, mountains, lakes, and oceans.

Smoke started to rise from the mountaintops.

Steam began to rise from the waters of the sea.

Poseidon, the god of the sea, rose up above the waves.

He shook his trident at the chariot.

But even the air grew too hot for him. Three times he dove into the water. Three times he rose again to shout at Phaeton. Still Phaeton came closer to the earth, like a shooting star.

The horses did not want to kill themselves.
So as they got closer to the earth,
they pulled up.
Now they were not going down anymore.
But they were not going up either.
They ran straight ahead,
towards the far western horizon.
As they galloped west,
trees and meadows caught fire.
Cities burned to the ground.
Rivers dried up.

As the chariot flew over Africa,
the great Sahara Forest caught fire.
This huge wooded area was burned
completely.

Even today it is still a hot, sandy place.
It is said that the people of Ethiopia
became black that day.

Phaeton looked
down upon the
world.
It felt like he was
breathing air from
a furnace.
He felt that he
would burn up.
He could not see through
the inky black smoke.
His eyes were filled with tears.
He had absolutely no control over
the chariot.

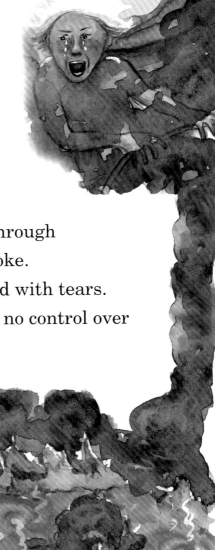

Creatures of the earth, beasts, men, even
the lesser gods, cried to Zeus for relief.
Demeter, the goddess of the earth pleaded,
"Oh, Zeus, the father of the gods,
why am I punished this way?
Do I deserve to die by fire?
Is this my reward for all the work I have
done? If I have angered you, why do you
not kill me with your thunderbolts?
At least let me die quickly by your hand."
"I have given life to all living beings.
I have supplied grass for cattle and fruit
for men. I have created wood and stone.
Without wood and stone, how could men
build temples to worship you and the other
gods?"

"But if you do not pity me, what about my
brother, the god of the sea?
He will soon dry up because of the heat."

5

ZEUS'S PUNISHMENT

It was Zeus's lightning bolt
that killed Phaeton.

"**P**lease Zeus, even if you do not want to spare us, think of your own heaven," said Demeter. "Already the North and South Pole are smoking. These are the poles that support your palace.

If they are destroyed, your palace will fall also. Atlas becomes weak under such heat. He can barely continue to hold me up." Demeter pleaded.

"If the earth, sea, and heaven disappear, we will fall back into ancient Chaos."

"Oh, Zeus! Save what is left of the earth, sea, and heaven.
Please do not wait anymore!
Take action, and relieve our pain quickly!"
Having said this, the earth was overcome with heat. Her throat was dry and her voice would not work.

Zeus felt the pain of the earth.
He saw the suffering of all living creatures.
He called all the other gods, including Apollo.
He told them that he would stop the destruction.

Then he climbed
the high tower
from where he
commanded the
weather.
But there were no
clouds on this day.

Mighty Zeus
roared.
Thunder came
from his mouth.
Lightning bolts
danced in his hand. Raising his arm,
he aimed a bolt at Phaeton.
A flash of white-hot light burned the sky.
A great crash echoed all over the earth.
The chariot burst into many pieces.
The horses ran home as Phaeton fell from
the sky.

50

Apollo's magic oil could not protect Phaeton
from one of Zeus's lightning bolts.
His body was burned and his hair was on fire.
His smoking body fell like a shooting star.
Phaeton fell into the river Eridanus.
Now all was quiet and dark.

Phaeton, Falling Into the River

Apollo was without a chariot.
He could not give the earth light and heat.
But as soon as the chariot fell to the earth,
Hephaestus started to make a new one.
He finished before Aurora awoke at the
start of the next day.

But Apollo
was sad at
the loss of
his son.
He would
not drive
the new
chariot.
He sat
alone and
sad in his
palace.

So the next day passed without sunlight.

Men and gods called to Zeus for help again.

"We need the sun back."

"We cannot live in the cold and dark."

Zeus and some other gods went to talk with
Apollo.

"You cannot leave the world in darkness,"
said Zeus.

But Apollo was angry at Zeus.

It was Zeus's lightning bolt that killed Phaeton.

Zeus spoke, "You lost a son. That is true.
But think of all the men, women, and
children who were killed.
If I had not acted, the
whole earth would have
disappeared in flames.
I had no choice."
Finally Apollo agreed
with Zeus.
He went to
get his
crown.

The next day, he tied
his horses to his new
chariot.
Then Aurora made
dawn appear in the
eastern sky.

Once again Apollo made his journey across
the sky.
He continues on his path even today.
From that day on, the sun will never go
too high or too low.

Reading Comprehension

● Read and answer the questions.

1. Choose the one thing that Phaeton didn't do during his journey.

   (A) He passed through India.
   (B) He saw many wonders.
   (C) He climbed mountains.
   (D) He explored the cities.

2. How did Phaeton's friends react when Phaeton said that he was Apollo's son?

   _____

   _____

3. Why didn't Phaeton stop walking except to eat and sleep during his journey?

   (A) Because he wanted to meet his father quickly.
   (B) Because he was not interested in the surroundings.
   (C) Because he was so tired.
   (D) Because he promised his mother.

4. What did Apollo offer Phaeton to prove that he was Phaeton's father?

_____

_____

5. How did Apollo try to persuade Phaeton?
   (A) He said that even Zeus would not drive the chariot.
   (B) He said that the chariot was too hot for Phaeton.
   (C) He said that Phaeton was not his son.
   (D) He said that Phaeton would be killed by the Great Bear and the Little Bear.

6. Apollo tried to scare Phaeton, but Phaeton was not afraid. Why?

_____

_____

7. What did the special oil do to the horses?

    (A) It made the horses' hooves more beautiful.
    (B) It enabled the horses to fly.
    (C) It made the horses grow bigger.
    (D) It made the horses breathe fire.

8. What was the final instruction Apollo gave his son about the horses?

    _____

    _____

9. What did Zeus's lightning bolt do to Phaeton?

    (A) It made Phaeton's body burst into many
        pieces.
    (B) It burned Phaeton's body.
    (C) It made him forget everything.
    (D) It made Phaeton change into a horse.

10. According to this story, why did the people of Ethiopia become black?

    _____

    _____

● Read and talk about it.

. . . To prove it, I will give you anything that you ask for. I swear it by the river Styx, which we gods swear by in our most solemn promises.
Phaeton immediately replied,
"I wish to drive your chariot, father." . . .
Your wish is too dangerous. . . . Apollo tried to persuade Phaeton. But he did not change his mind. . . .

11. Apollo gave Phaeton his chariot, and Phaeton died. What would you have done if you were Apollo?

_____

_____

. . . Apollo tried to persuade Phaeton. But he did not change his mind.
. . . "I fear that my gift will kill you," said Apollo.
Phaeton listened, but he was not afraid. He wanted to show the world that he was really Apollo's son. . . .

12. Why didn't Phaeton think of another way to prove Apollo was his father?
    How would you show the world that you were the son of Apollo, if you were Phaeton?

_____

_____

The Signs of the Zodiac

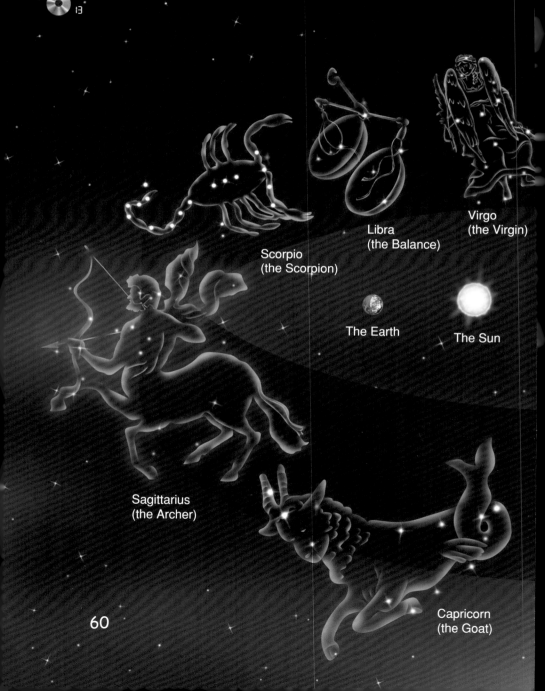

Scorpio
(the Scorpion)

Libra
(the Balance)

Virgo
(the Virgin)

The Earth

The Sun

Sagittarius
(the Archer)

Capricorn
(the Goat)

The word "zodiac" comes from a Greek word meaning,
"the circle of animals"
Where did the zodiac come from?
In this section, you can find the Greek Myths
that explain the origins of these signs.

Leo
(the Lion)

Cancer
(the Crab)

Gemini
(the Twins)

Taurus
(the Bull)

Aries
(the Ram)

Pisces
(the Fishes)

Aquarius
(the Water Bearer)

61

Aries (the Ram)
March 21st ~ April 20th

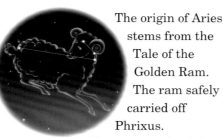

The origin of Aries stems from the Tale of the Golden Ram. The ram safely carried off Phrixus.

Phrixus sacrificed the Golden Ram to Zeus and in turn, Zeus placed the ram in the heavens.

Taurus (the Bull)
April 21st ~ May 20th

The origin of Taurus stems from the Tale of Europa and the Bull.
Zeus turned himself into a bull in order to attract Europa to him.
The bull carried Europa across the sea to Crete.
In remembrance, Zeus placed the image of the bull in the stars.

Gemini (the Twins)
May 21st ~ June 21st

This sign stems from the Tale of Castor and Pollux. Castor and Pollux were twins. They both loved each other very much. In honor of the brothers's great love, Zeus placed them among the stars.

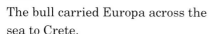

Cancer (the Crab)
June 22nd ~ July 22nd

The sign of Cancer stems from one of the 12 Labors of Hercules.

Hera sent the crab to kill Hercules. But Hercules crushed the crab under his foot just before he defeated the Hydra. To honor the crab, Hera placed it among the stars.

Leo (the Lion)
July 23rd ~ August 22nd

The sign of Leo stems from another of Hercules 12 Labors. Hercules's first labor was to kill a lion that lived in Nemea valley. He killed the Nemea lion with his hands. In remembrance of the grand battle, Zeus placed the Lion of Nemea among the stars.

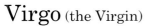

 18

Libra (the Balance)
September 23rd ~ October 21st

The Libra are the scales that balance justice. They are held by the goddess of divine justice, Themis. Libra shines right beside Virgo which represents Astraea, daughter of Themis.

Virgo (the Virgin)
August 23rd ~ September 22nd

Virgo's origin stems from the Tale of Pandora. Virgo represents the goddess of purity and innocence, Astraea. After Pandora opened the

forbidden box and let loose all the evils into the world, every god went back to heaven. As a remembrance of innocence lost, Astraea was placed amongst the stars in the form of Virgo.

Scorpio (the Scorpion)
October 22nd ~ November 21st

The sign of Scorpio stems from the Tale of Orion. Orion and Artemis were great hunting partners, which made Artemis's brother Apollo very jealous. Apollo pleaded with Gaea to kill Orion. So Gaea created the scorpion and killed great Orion. In remembrance of this act, Zeus placed Orion and the scorpion amongst the stars. But they never appear at the same time.

Sagittarius(the Archer)

November 23rd ~ December 21st

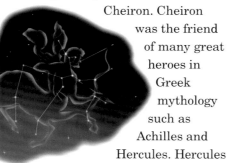

This sign is representative of Cheiron. Cheiron was the friend of many great heroes in Greek mythology such as Achilles and Hercules. Hercules accidentally shot Cheiron in the leg with a poison arrow. Cheiron was immortal so he couldn't die. Instead, he had to endure the unending pain. Cheiron begged Zeus to kill him. To honor Cheiron, Zeus placed him among the stars.

 19

Capricorn(the Goat)

December 22nd ~ January 19th

The sign of Capricorn represents the goat Amalthea who fed the infant Zeus. It's said that Zeus placed her among the stars in gratitude.

Aquarius
(the Water Bearer)

January 20th ~ February 18th

The sign of Aquarius stems from the Tale of Deucalion's Flood. In this tale, Zeus pours all the waters of the heavens onto earth to wash away all the evil creatures. Deucalion and his wife Pyrrha were the only survivors of the great flood.

Pisces(the Fishes)

February 19th ~ March 20th

The Pisces represents the goddess of love & beauty, Aphrodite and her son the god of love, Eros. They were taking a stroll down the Euphrates River when there was a typhoon. They pleaded for Zeus to help them escape, so Zeus changed them into fish and they swam away safely. In remembrance of this, Aphrodite is the big fish constellation and Eros is the small fish constellation.

Apollo's Chariot

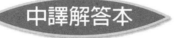

中譯解答本

卓加真　譯

神話以趣味的方式，為我們生活中的煩惱提出解釋，並滿足我們的好奇心。許多故事的編寫，都是為了解釋一些令人驚奇或恐懼的現象，因此，世界各地不同的國家、民族，都有屬於自己的神話。

希臘與羅馬神話充滿想像力，並結合了諸神與英雄們激盪人心的傳奇故事，因此特別為人所津津樂道。希臘與羅馬神話反應了真實的人類世界，因此，閱讀神話對於瞭解西方文化與思維，有極大的幫助。

這些經典故事的背景，可追溯至史前時代，但對於當代的讀者而言，它們深具魅力的法寶何在？其秘密就在於，神話能超越時空，完整地呈現人類心中的慾望。這些激盪人心的冒險故事，將帶您經歷生命中的各種重要事件：戰爭與和平、生命與死亡、善與惡，以及各種愛恨情仇。

希臘與羅馬神話裡所描繪的諸神，並不全是完美、萬能的天神，他們和人類一樣，會因憤怒而打鬥，會耍詭計戲弄其他天神，會因愛與嫉妒而感到痛苦。在 Let's Enjoy Mythology 系列的第二部 Reading Greek and Roman Mythology in English 中，你將會讀到許多具有人類特質的英雄、女英雄、眾神和女神的故事。

Reading Greek and Roman Mythology in English 將引領你穿越時空，一探想像中的古希臘世界。

前言

　　費頓是太陽神阿波羅和水澤女神克里夢妮之子，自己的父親竟是阿波羅，讓他非常引以為傲。不過，費頓的玩伴們不相信，他們嘲笑他，要他證明自己的確是阿波羅的兒子。最後，他決定出發去找阿波羅太陽神，向全世界證明他和阿波羅是父子關係。於是，有生以來，他終於第一次見到了自己的父親。

　　阿波羅承諾他，會答應他的任何要求，好讓他可以證明自己的確就是太陽神之子。他於是大大地做了一個要求：他說，他要駕駛阿波羅的馬車，而這個輛馬車除了阿波羅之外，沒有人有能力駕馭。駕駛阿波羅馬車是非常危險的事，連眾神之王宙斯也不願一試。但阿波羅無法拒絕費頓的要求，因為他是對著守誓河起誓來承諾費頓的。

　　阿波羅百般地勸費頓要放棄這個念頭，但費頓聽不進去，直上了馬車駕駛了起來。最後，他終於闖了大禍。就如阿波羅所告誡的，他是無法駕馭馬匹的。馬匹後來失控，飛離了原本在天際的軌道，為諸神的天上和人類的地上帶來了橫禍。費頓駕著馬車摔落，至今還影響著我們現今的生活嗎？你能想像當時候所發生的狀況嗎？

目録

1
費頓，阿波羅之子

「你要真的是阿波羅之子，
就證明給我們看啊！」

p. 8

在古代衣索匹亞，
住著一位名為費頓的男孩。
他母親是一位
名為克里夢妮的水澤女神，
他父親是太陽神阿波羅。

- **ancient** [ˈeɪnʃənt]
  古代的；古老的
- **Ethiopia**
  衣索匹亞（東非國家）
- **nymph** [nɪmf]
  山林水澤女神（希神）

- -

p. 9

有一天，費頓和玩伴們玩耍，
他吹噓道：「我爸爸是太陽神。」
但玩伴們譏笑他，挑釁地說道：
「你爸爸才不是太陽神呢！
因為你爸爸不想娶妳媽媽，
你媽媽就說這種話來騙人，
結果你竟然相信，真是蠢呀。
你要真的是阿波羅之子，
那就證明給我們看啊！」

- **was playing with**
  [wɑːz ˈpleɪɪŋ wɪθ]
  與……玩耍
- **boast** [boʊst] 自吹自擂
- **tease** [tiːz] 取笑；欺負
- **by saying** [baɪ ˈseɪɪŋ]
  以言論
- **make up** [meɪk ʌp] 虛構
- **foolish** [ˈfuːlɪʃ]
  愚蠢的；傻的
- **prove** [pruːv] 證明

p. 10

但費頓無法證明，
只能帶著疑惑和羞辱回家。

一回到家，他馬上來到母親面前。
「媽咪，我真是太陽神之子嗎？
沒人相信我的話。」
克里夢妮嘆息著說：
「孩子啊，我要是說謊騙你，
就讓太陽來取走我的性命吧。
你的父親，的的確確
就是賜予人類溫暖和陽光的太陽。」

- **proof** [pru:f] 證據
- **confused** [kənˋfju:zd] 困惑的
- **ashamed** [əˋʃeɪmd] 羞愧的
- **as soon as** 一……就
- **sigh** [saɪ] 嘆息；嘆氣
- **warmth** [wɔ:rmθ] 溫暖
- **light** [laɪt] 光

p. 11

「我也只能這樣跟你說，
無法證明什麼。
你要是不相信，
你可以去問你的父親阿波羅呀！
他的神廟就在東邊的山裡頭。」
費頓聽見母親的建議，感到欣喜不已。

當晚，他睡得特別香甜，
早已打包好一路上所需要的行李。

- **why don't you**
  你何不……
- **edge** [edʒ] 邊緣
- **on the eastern edge of**
  在極東之境
- **the land** 土地
- **overjoyd** [ˋouvə(r)dʒɔɪd] 狂喜的
- **prepare** [prɪˋper] 準備
- **journey** [ˋdʒɜ:rni] 旅程
- **sleep** [sli:p] 睡覺
- **soundly** [ˋsaundli] 酣然地

p. 12

隔天早晨，他告別母親，
往旭日東昇之處出發。
他經過印度，
看到許多驚奇的事物。
有時候，
他也想佇足探索途中的城市，
與當地人交談，
但他有要務在身。

- **say goodbye to**
  向……道別
- **the rising sun**
  冉冉上升的太陽；朝陽
- **toward** [təˋɔ:rd] 朝……
- **through** [θru:] 穿過
- **India** 印度
- **wonder** [ˋwʌndə(r)]
  奇妙的；不可思議的
- **explore** [ɪkˋsplɔ:(r)] 探險
- **goal** [goʊl] 目標；方向

 p. 13

他一天一天走向父親，
除了吃飯睡覺，
他從不停下腳步。

他只花了一個星期的時間，
便來到了極東之境。
他走進山中，累得睡著了。

- **got closer to**
  向……接近
- **except** [ɪkˋsept]
  除了……之外
- **it take** 花費（時間）
- **climb** [klaɪm] 爬
- **fall asleep** [fɔ:l əˋsli:p]
  近入睡眠

2
太陽神阿波羅

阿波羅微笑著，緊緊擁抱兒子。

 p. 14

隔天早上，太陽還未昇起，
費頓便醒來。
他看到奇怪的光芒，
便攀爬上陡峭山坡，看見了一間宮殿。
他當下就明白了，
這就是太陽神阿波羅的神殿。

神殿由金與銅鑄造而成，
莊嚴無比！
高聳的白色大理石柱支撐著建築，
白色的階梯一路延伸至大門，
入口處是兩扇巨大閃亮的金色門扉。

- **before dawn**
  [brɪˈfɔ:(r) dɔ:n]
  黎明破曉前
- **strange** [streɪndʒ]
  奇異的
- **steep** [sti:p] 陡峭的
- **immediately** [ɪˈmi:diətli]
  直接地；立刻地
- **be made of**
  由……製成的
- **bronze** [brɑ:nz] 青銅
- **amazing** [əˈmeɪzɪŋ]
  令人吃驚的
- **marble** [ˈmɑ:rbl] 大理石
- **column** [ˈkɑ:ləm] 圓柱
- **support** [səˈpɔ:rt] 支撐
- **entire** [ɪnˈtaɪə(r)]
  全部的；整個的
- **staircase** [ˈsterkeɪs] 樓梯
- **lead** [li:d] 通向
- **lead up to** 通向至……
- **huge** [hju:dʒ]
  巨大的；龐大的
- **shining** [ˈʃaɪnɪŋ] 光亮的
- **entrance** [ˈentrəns]
  入口；門口

p. 15

費頓開始走上階梯。
快走到底時，
他看到鑲刻在神殿牆上的圖案。
赫發斯特斯是眾神的工匠，
這間神殿就是他所建造的。
他將地上、水中、天上的圖像，
都刻在牆上。

- **carve on** [kɑːrv ɑːn]
  雕刻在……上
- **Hephaestus** 赫發斯特斯
  (希神；火神)
- **master** [ˈmæstə(r)]
  能手；大師
- **craftsman** [ˈkræftsmən]
  工匠；巧匠

---

p. 16

費頓來到階梯末端，
銀色的巨大門扉打開了。
他走進神殿，進入一個大房間。
他在這一頭就停下腳步，
因為有很明亮的光線，
讓他無法看清楚。

這是太陽神阿波羅的大廳。
眼前這一幕，讓費頓看得很訝異。
在另一頭的寶座上，就坐著太陽神。
他穿著一件紫色袍子，
頭上戴著冠冕，

- **go inside** 走進裡面
- **enter** [ˈentə(r)] 進入
- **stop** [stɑːp] 停下
- **at a distance**
  在一距離之外
- **couldn't see well**
  無法看清
- **hall** [hɔːl] 大廳
- **amazing** [əˈmeɪzɪŋ]
  令人吃驚的
- **throne** [θroʊn]
  王位；寶座

冠冕閃耀著太陽的光芒，
看起來好像是由純淨的白光所形成的。
阿波羅的寶座，
也因兩旁鑲嵌著無數的寶石，
而金光閃閃。

- at the far end
  在遠處一端
- sat [sæt] 坐
  （sit的過去式）
- wore [wɔːr] 戴
  （wear的過去式）
- purple [ˋpɜːrpl] 紫色的
- robe [roʊb] 袍子
- crown [kraʊn] 王冠
- shone with [ʃoʊn wɪθ]
  閃耀著……（shone是
  shine的過去式）
- seem [siːm] 似乎
- glitter [ˋɡlɪtə(r)]
  閃閃發光

p. 18

因為白光太刺眼，
費頓先看了寶座兩邊的眾神。
在阿波羅的右邊，
站著年神、月神、日神；
在他左邊，則站了四季眾神

- hurt [hɜːrt] 傷害
- look at 看著……
- on both sides of
  在……的兩側

p. 19

春之神是位年輕的金髮女神，
身著翡翠綠袍。
花朵似乎從她髮際長出，
遮蓋著整個身體。

站在她旁邊的是夏之神。
她是位稍長的黑髮女神，
戴著穀類所製的冠冕。

- **yellow-haired**
  [ˈjelou ˌherd] 黃色頭髮的
- **bright** [braɪt] 光亮的
- **grow down** [grou daun]
  垂長下來
- **cover** [ˈkʌvər] 覆蓋
- **beside** [bɪˈsaɪd]
  在……附近
- **slightly** [ˈslaɪtli] 稍微地
- **dark-haired**
  [ˈdɑːrk ˌherd]
  深色頭髮的
- **grain** [greɪn] 穀粒

 p. 20

接下來是中年的秋之神，
有著灰褐的髮色。
他穿著的長袍，
由橘黃、緋紅的樹葉所組成。
他的雙腳，染著葡萄汁液，
手中握著一串葡萄。

- **a middle-aged**
  [ə ˈmɪdl ˌeɪdʒd] 中年的
- **bare** [ber] 赤裸的
- **were stained with**
  [wə(r) steɪnd wɪð]
  被……沾染了
- **bunch** [bʌntʃ] 串

最後是年老的冬之神。
他雪白的頭髮和鬍鬚，
被冰霜凍得好像帶著藍色，
而且像冰柱一樣僵直。

- **beard** [bɪrd] 鬍子
- **blue** [blu:] 藍色的
- **frost** [frɔ:st] 霜
- **stiff** [stɪf] 僵直的；硬的
- **icicle** [ˋaɪsɪkl] 冰柱

p. 21

阿波羅一眼認出自己的兒子，
說話時，太陽神的雙眼像火般耀眼。
「費頓，
你怎麼來到這麼遠的世界東邊來了？」
「偉大的阿波羅神啊，
願您真是我父親，
我來，就是為了想證實此事。」
阿波羅微笑，緊緊抱住兒子。

- **at first sight**
  [æt fɜ:rst saɪt] 第一眼
- **recognize** [ˋrekəgnaɪz]
  認出
- **blaze** [bleɪz] 閃耀著
- **smile** [smaɪl]
  微笑
- **gently** [ˋdʒentli] 溫柔地
- **hug tightly**
  [hʌg ˋtaɪtli] 緊緊地抱住

3
費頓的願望

「我希望能夠駕駛你的馬車，
父親。」

p. 22

阿波羅脫下刺眼的冠冕放在一旁。
「你母親說的是真的，
我的確就是你的父親。
為了要讓你證明，
我會答應你的一切要求。
我就對著守誓河起誓，
眾神都是在那裡立下重誓的。」
費頓立即回答，
「我希望能夠駕駛你的馬車，父親。」
「不行，孩子，
請你換個願望，任何願望都行，
但這一個願望太危險了，
就連眾神之父宙斯，
也無法駕馭太陽馬車。」

- **take off** [teɪk ɔ:f]
  取下；拿下
- **swear** [swer] 發誓
- **the river Styx**
  [ðə ˈrɪvə(r) stɪks] 守誓河
- **solemn** [ˈsɑ:ləm]
  莊重的；嚴肅的
- **chariot** [ˈtʃærɪət]
  （古代的）雙輪戰車
- **something else**
  [ˈsʌmθɪŋ els]
  其他事物
- **anything but that**
  [ˈenɪθɪŋ bʌt ðæt]
  任何事物除了……
- **dangerous**
  [ˈdeɪndʒərəs]
  危險的

p. 23

「馬車對你來說會太熱了，
馬匹也會噴火，牠們很悍，
連我要駕馭牠們都不是很簡單的事。
我很抱歉發下這樣的誓言，
請你另外選個願望。」
阿波羅想勸退費頓，
但費頓不想改變心意。

- **too** [tu:] 太……
- **breathe fire**
  [bri:ð `faɪə(r)] 噴火
- **difficult** [`dɪfɪkəlt]
  困難的
- **control** [kən`troul] 控制
- **make a promise to**
  [meɪk ə `prɑ:mɪs tu:]
  向……許下承諾
- **persuade** [pər`sweɪd]
  說明

---

p. 24

阿波羅想嚇阻費頓。
「我對著守誓河起誓，
不能違背承諾。
但孩子，請小心，
天際之途，驚險萬分，
上坡途中，路途陡峭。
你將昇上高空，
千萬不要往下望，
不然會因暈眩而跌落的！」

- **scare** [sker] 驚恐
- **break promise**
  [breɪk `prɑ:mɪs]
  打破承諾
- **beware** [bɪ`wer]
  當心；小心
- **be full of danger**
  [bi fʊl ʌv `deɪndʒə(r)]
  充滿危險
- **steep** [sti:p] 陡峭的
- **look down** [lʊk daʊn]
  往下看
- **dizzy** [`dɪzi] 頭暈目眩的

13

p. 25

「你飛在天上時，
不會看到眾神的住所，
祂們住在更高的地方。不過，
你會經過住在星辰之間的可怕怪物，
那是壯碩的金牛座。
小心它頭上的角！
也要注意射手的箭！」
阿波羅警告著。

- **terrible** [ˋterəbl]
  可怕的；嚇人的
- **Taurus** [ˋtɔ:rəs] 金牛座
- **mighty** [ˋmaɪtɪ]
  強大的；有力的
- **horn** [hɔ:rn] 角
- **arrow** [ˋærou] 箭
- **Archer** [ˋa:rtʃə(r)]

---

 p. 26

「兇猛的獅子座會為你開路，
它有尖銳的爪子和牙齒，
你也會在巨蟹座和天蠍座的毒爪之間
穿梭而過。

你要小心巨蠍的毒針，
它會發出很強的毒液。
如果被巨蠍螫到了，
就會悽慘地慢慢死去。
在這所有的期間，
天空也會緩緩地翻轉著，
你一定要特別留意。」阿波羅說。

- **Leo** [ˋli:ou] 獅子座
- **fierce** [fɪrs]
  兇猛的；殘酷的
- **sharp** [ʃa:rp] 鋒利的
- **claw** [klɔ:] 爪
- **teeth** [ti:θ] 牙齒（複數）
- **between A and B**
  在A和B之間
- **Scorpion** [ˋskɔ:rpiən]
  天蠍座
- **horrible** [ˋhɔ:rəbl]
  令人毛骨悚然的
- **poison** [ˋpɔɪzn] 有毒的
- **all the while** [ɔ:l ðə waɪl]
  在此同時
- **pay attention**
  [peɪ əˋtenʃn] 注意；留心

14

p. 27

「而就算通過了星辰天際，
也還不算安全。
最困難的部分是下坡，
下坡和上坡一樣陡，
要用上一切技巧才不至失控。
海洋女神蒂賽絲，
總會在另一邊等著我，
因爲她擔心我會摔落。
而你只是個凡人，
我擔心這個禮物會奪走你的性命。」
阿波羅說。

〔圖〕阿波羅與馬車

- **even if** [ˋiːvn ɪf] 即使
- **not . . . yet** 尚未
- **the most difficult**
  [ðə moʊst ˋdɪfɪkəlt]
  最困難的
- **as steep as**
  如……一般陡峭
- **require** [rɪˋkwaɪə(r)] 需要
- **Tethys** 海洋女神蒂賽絲
- **wait for** [weɪt fə(r)]
  等待……
- **on the other side**
  在另一邊
- **mortal** [ˋmɔːrtl] 致命的
- **fear** [fɪr] 害怕
- **gift** [gɪft] 禮物

p. 28

費頓聽著，卻絲毫不退縮。
他想要向全世界證明，
他確是阿波羅之子。
黎明時刻愈來愈逼近，
阿波羅嘆息著，
帶著兒子來到大馬車旁。
這輛神奇馬車，
是赫發斯特斯送的禮物，
由純金與純銀所打造。

- **listen** [ˋlɪsn] 聆聽
- **the world** [ðə wɜːld]
  這個世界
- **sunrise** [ˋsʌnraɪz] 日出
- **was getting near**
  越來越接近……
- **take . . . to . . .**
  帶領……前往
- **vehicle** [ˋviːhɪkl]
  運載工具；車輛
- **solid gold** [ˋsɑːlɪd goʊld]
  純金的

15

p. 29

整輛馬車金光閃閃，
點綴在座椅上的是各種寶石，
有紅寶石、綠寶石還有鑽石。
這光芒與阿波羅的冠冕，相映輝煌。
二十四位年輕女神羅列在旁，
分別代表一天二十四個小時，
她們的工作是負責備馬。

- **brightly** [ˋbraɪtlɪ] 明亮地
- **along** [əˋlɔ:ŋ] 沿著
- **gem** [dʒem] 寶石；寶玉
- **such as** 如此⋯⋯的
- **hit** [hɪt] 到達
- **sparkle** [ˋspɑr:kl] 閃耀
- **stand by** 站在一旁

p. 30

兩匹白馬以巨蹄踹踏地面。
牠們的蹄上抹著特殊油脂，
能讓牠們飛天。
白馬迫不及待開始每日的行程，
費頓站在馬車邊，
可以感受到馬匹呼出的熱氣。

- **pair of** 一雙⋯⋯
- **struck the ground with** 以⋯⋯擊地（struck 是 strike 的過去式）
- **hooves** [hu:vz] 蹄（單數形為 hoof）
- **were coated with** 被塗抹上⋯⋯
- **allow . . . to** 允許⋯⋯去
- **seem anxious to** 似乎急著地想⋯⋯
- **heat** [hi:t] 熱氣

p. 31

頃刻間，

黑暗的天際變得如玫瑰色斑斕，

曙光女神奧羅拉已揭開宮殿的幕廉。

每個早晨，

從女神床邊迸射出的晨曦曙光，

便象徵新的一天即將開始。

阿波羅做最後嘗試：

「馬車就要開始行程，

但改變心意還來得及，

兒子，聽我的話，

不要執意這樣做。」

然而費頓打定了主意，

馬匹和金黃馬車讓他覺得很神氣，

他還不知道要害怕它們恐怖的力量。

- **suddenly** [ˈsʌdənli]
  突然地
- **darkness** [ˈdɑːrknəs]
  黑暗
- **become rosy**
  [bɪˈkʌm ˈrouzi]
  變成玫瑰色的
- **Aurora** [ɔˈrɔːrə]
  曙光女神賓羅拉
- **curtain** [ˈkɜːrtn] 帘幕
- **signal** [ˈsɪgnəl] 打信號
- **pride** [praɪd]
  自豪；得意

p. 32

阿波羅從時間女神那裡取來一個罐子，
從中倒出金油，
把它們抹在費頓的頭髮和臉上。
「兒子，這神奇金油會保護你，
以免被冠冕給灼傷了。」
說罷，便把光之冠冕戴在費頓的頭上。
這一次，強光不再讓費頓睜不開眼。
阿波羅最後一次叮嚀兒子。
「千萬不要鞭打馬匹要牠們走快一點，
而且牠們自己不會慢下來，
記住，你一定要使勁全身力氣
緊抓住韁繩。」

- **jar** [dʒɑ:(r)] 罐
- **pour** [pɔ:(r)] 倒；灌；注
- **protect** [prəˋtekt] 保護
- **final** [ˋfaɪnl] 最後的
- **instruction** [ɪnˋstrʌkʃən] 教學
- **slow down** [sloʊ daʊn] 慢下來；緩下來
- **by oneself** [baɪ wʌnˋself] 獨自一人的
- **hold onto the rein** 緊抓住韁繩
- **with all . . . strength** 用盡……的力氣

p. 33

「千萬別讓韁繩滑開！
韁繩一鬆，就無法控制馬車，
這樣對天庭和人間，都會釀成大災難。
你要是駛得太高，
會燒到天神的住處；
你要是駛得太低，
會燒死人類和動物。

- **slip** [slɪp] 滑動；滑行
- **lose control of** [lu:z kənˋtroʊl ʌv] 失去輚……的控制
- **the safest** 最安全的 (safe安全的；safer較安全的)
- **proper** [ˋprɑ:pə(r)] 適合的；適當的

駛在中間，才是最佳的安全之路，
這樣才會給予天庭和人間
適當的光與熱。
循著我每日所行駛過的軌跡來走，
可以幫忙引導道路。」

- **proper amount of**
  [ˈprɑːpə(r) əˈmaʊnt ʌv]
  適當的……
- **follow** [ˈfɑːloʊ] 跟隨
- **wheel mark** [wiːl mɑːrk]
  車輪軌跡
- **left** [left] 留下
  （leave的過去式）
- **day after day**
  日復一日
- **guide** [gaɪd] 引導；帶領

---

p. 34

一位時間女神將紫色門扉打開，
以紅玫瑰花瓣灑在道路上。
在另一頭的西邊遠方，
阿波羅可以看見妹妹月亮女神。
她剛剛結束在天際的行程，
天空中的群星正隨著晨星離開，
待晨星消失，太陽便要上場了。

- **push open**
  [pʊʃ ˈoʊpən] 推開
- **pathway** [ˈpæθweɪ]
  路；小徑
- **far away** [fɑː(r) əˈweɪ]
  遠遠地
- **the Moon** [ðə muːn]
  月亮女神
- **were being led away**
  隨……離開
- **the morning star**
  晨星（通常指金星，
  evening star晚星，通常
  指木星或水星）
- **was supposed to**
  原被認定為……
- **disappear** [dɪsəˈpɪə(r)]
  消失；不見

4
太陽馬車上之費頓

他拉緊韁繩，
但馬匹毫不為所動。

p. 35

費頓跳上馭馬座位，
一位時間女神將韁繩交給他。
費頓取過韁繩，
馬匹揚起牠們的頭，
大門打開，
馬匹噴出火焰與濃煙，向前奔跑。
費頓感覺馬車向前躍進，
一時還真像馬車也是活的一樣。
馬匹前進，在雲間開路。
牠們強有力的雙腿，
奮力踏在路途上。

〔圖〕馬車上的費頓

- **jump up** [dʒʌp ʌp]
  跳起來；躍起
- **offer** [`ɔ:fə(r)] 提供
- **lift** [lɪft] 抬起；舉起
- **snort** [snɔ:rt] 噴鼻息
- **moved forward**
  [mu:v `fɔ:rwərd]
  向前行；向前移動
- **leap** [li:p] 跳；躍
- **for a second**
  [fɔ:(r) ə `sekənd]
  在一瞬間
- **imagine** [ɪ`mædʒɪn]
  想像
- **alive** [ə`laɪv]
  活著的；有生命的
- **pound** [paʊnd]
  （連續）猛擊

p. 36

剛開始，費頓非常興奮。
然而馬兒覺得車子重量減輕，
知道駕馬之人力道不足，
便更是加快腳步，狂野飛奔，

- **at first** [ət fɜ:rst] 一開始
- **excited** [ɪk`saɪtɪd] 興奮的
- **load** [loʊd]
  （馬車的）裝載量
- **lighter** [`laɪtə(r)]
  較輕的（light輕的；
  lightest最輕的）
- **weaker** [`wi:kə(r)]
  較弱（weak弱的；
  weakest最輕的）

使得馬車搖搖晃晃的。

這時，費頓才開始後悔自己的選擇。

他拉緊韁繩，但馬匹毫不爲所動。

沒多久，馬匹駛離道路，

飛奔在天際。

- **wilder** [ˋwaɪldə(r)]
  較野的；較難以駕馭的
  （wild 野的；
  wildes 最野的）
- **from side to side**
  從一側到另一側
- **regret** [rɪˋgrɛt] 後悔
- **pull** [pʊl] 拉
- **ignore** [ɪgˋnɔː(r)] 忽視
- **ran off** [ræn ɔːf] 跑離；
  駛離（ran 是 run 的過去式）
- **wide-open** [ˋwaɪd ˏoʊpən]
  完全開放的

---

p. 37

太陽光線從東邊升起，

但是光線沒有轉強，

反而越來越黯淡，因爲馬匹越走越高！

沒多久，太陽光消失不見了，

從黎明的曙光，又變回黑夜！

地上的人類感到很疑惑，

才剛看到新的一天，

卻又馬上消失！

太陽變得只像黑空中的一顆行星！

- **rose** [roʊz] 升起
  （rise 的過去式）
- **instead of** [ɪnˋstɛd ʌv]
  取而代之的
- **getting stronger**
  [ˋgɛtɪŋ ˋstrɔːgə(r)]
  越來越強
- **become weaker**
  變得更弱了
- **turn back into**
  變回成爲……
- **confused** [kənˋfjuːzd]
  困惑的；疑惑的
- **promise** [ˋprɑːmɪs]
- **inky** [ˋɪŋki] 如墨水的

21

p. 38

太陽神的馬車駛向北極星，
當馬車一接近，北極就熱了起來。
住在北極的魔蛇，
第一次感到太陽的熱力。
牠因為在冬眠，
已經有好長一段時間沒有活動了，
但現在，牠被熱醒起來，
發出嘶嘶聲地吐著氣，
讓牠的毒氣因此瀰漫整個北極。

- **the North Star**
  [ðə nɔːrθ stɑː(r)] 北極星
- **the North Pole**
  [ðə nɔːrθ poʊl] 北極
- **The Serpent**
  [ðə ˋsɜːrpənt] 巨蛇；魔蛇
- **lay around** [leɪ əˋraʊnd]
  躺在……附近
  （lay是lie的過去式）
- **for the first time**
  第一次
- **for a long time**
  持續了一段時間
- **hiss** [hɪs]
  （蛇）發出嘶嘶聲
- **poisonous** [ˋpɔɪzənəs]
  有毒的

- -

p. 39

天空中的星座，
也都紛紛感受到了熱氣。
大熊和小熊熱得受不了，
覺得好像要著火一樣，
真希望自己能夠跳到海裡頭去。

- **creature** [ˋkriːtʃə(r)]
  生物
- **the Great Bear**
  大熊星座
- **the Little Bear**
  小熊星座

p. 40

費頓望下看，一陣暈眩。
大地在他腳下，越變越小。
他臉色蒼白，雙腳發軟。
他盡量不去往下看，
但他還是一樣害怕。
這時他見到一幅可怕的景象，
馬匹正駛向巨蠍的方向！
這隻巨大的怪獸，正甩起尾巴，
他可以看到從毒針滴下的毒液。
接著，他聞到毒液的味道，
令他肚子一陣翻絞。

- **stand** [stænd]
  忍受；經得起
- **jump into** 跳進

- **shook** [ʃuk] 抖動
  （shake的過去式）
- **terror** [ˋterə(r)]
  恐怖；驚駭
- **relief** [rɪˋliːf]
  解救；補助
- **ahead** [əˋhed] 在前頭
- **a horrible sight**
  [ə ˋhɔːrəbl saɪt]
  一個恐怖的景象
- **drip** [ˋdrɪp] 滴下
- **stinger** [ˋstɪɡə(r)]
  有刺的動物

p. 41

他鬆開韁繩，抓住馬車，
馬匹知道韁繩鬆了，
便突然往地面直直俯衝下去。
牠們越跑越接近地面，
費頓可以看見河川、山脈、
湖泊和海洋。
山頂開始冒起濃煙，
海面上也出現蒸汽。

- **drop the reins**
  [drɑːp ðə reɪns]
  丟下韁繩
- **held onto** [held `ɑ:ntə]
  抓在……之上（held是
  hold的過去式）
- **plunge** [plʌndʒ]
  使突然前傾
- **closer and closer**
  越來越接近
- **rise from** [raɪz frʌm]
  從……升起
- **steam** [sti:m] 蒸汽

---

p. 42

海神波賽墩從海中出現，
對著馬車揮舞著他的三叉戟。
但空氣實在熱得令他受不了，
他就這樣躲進水中三次，又浮出海面，
對著費頓咆哮。
費頓沒有停下，
他宛如一顆流星般，
向地面俯衝下去。

- **trident** [`traɪdnt] 三叉戟
- **dove** [doʊv] 潛水
  （dive的過去式）
- **shout at** 對……呼喊；
  對……叫嚷
- **shooting star**
  [`ʃuːtɪŋ stɑː(r)] 流星

p. 43

但馬匹還想活，
就在接近地面的瞬間，
牠們將馬車往上拉了起來。
馬車這時駛得不上也不下，
平平直直駛向遠方西邊的地平線。
它們所經路線途中，
樹木和草地都著了火，
城市燒成灰燼，
河水乾涸。

- **pull up** [pʊl ʌp]
  向上拉起
- **horizon** [həˋraɪzn]
  地平線
- **gallop** [ˋgæləp] 疾馳
- **meadow** [ˋmɛdoʊ]
  草地；牧草地
- **catch fire** [kætʃ ˋfaɪə(r)]
  起火了
- **burn to** 延燒至……
- **dried up** [draɪd ʌp] 乾涸
  （dried 是 dry 的過去式）

---

p. 44

當馬車飛越非洲時，
大撒哈拉森林也燒了起來，
一大片森林完全成為灰燼。

時至今日，
這裡仍然是一個炎熱、多沙的地方。
據說，衣索比亞人也是在那天
變得全身黑皮膚的。

- **forest** [ˋfɔ:rɪst] 森林
- **wooded** [ˋwʊdɪd]
  樹林繁茂的
- **sandy place**
  [ˋsændi pleɪs]
  漠地；沙漠
- **Ethiopia**
  衣索比亞

p. 45

費頓俯瞰世界，
他感覺自己在呼吸著火爐的熱氣，
感覺自己就快要燒起來了。
他的視線被黑色的濃煙給擋住，
眼睛被熏得眼淚直流。
現在，他對馬車已完全失去控制。

- **furnace** [ˈfɜːrnɪs] 熔爐
- **absolutely** [ˈæbsəluːtli] 絕對地；完全地
- **have no control over** 對……失去控制

 p. 46

地上的生物、畜生和人類，
甚至連較小的神祉，
都向宙斯呼喊求救。
農業女神狄蜜特向宙斯請求道，
「眾神之父，宙斯，
我為何遭受如此嚴酷之懲罰？
我難道應該被火燒死嗎？
這是我一切心血所應得的報酬嗎？
如果我觸怒了你，
你何不用你的雷霆直接將我劈死？
至少讓我求個好死。」

- **lesser** [ˈlesə(r)] 較小的
- **for relief** [fɔː(r) rɪˈliːf] 為求解救
- **plead** [pliːd] 懇求
- **deserve** [dɪˈzɜːrv] 應受；該得
- **reward** [rɪˈwɔːrd] 報償

「我是賜予萬物生命的神，
我為牛群提供草地，
為人類提供果實；
我創造森林和岩石，
若非如此，
人類如何能建設神殿
祭拜你和其他神祉呢？」

「若你不憐憫我，
至少想想我的兄弟海神，
大海即將因熱氣而乾涸。」

- **thunderbolt**
  [ˈθʌndərboʊlt] 雷霆
- **at least** 至少
- **supply . . . for**
  [səˈplaɪ fə(r)]
  為……提供……
- **cattle** [ˈkætl] 牛
- **grass** [græs] 草
- **temple** [ˈtempl] 神殿
- **worship** [ˈwɜːrʃɪp] 戰爭
- **dry up** [draɪ ʌp] 乾涸
- **because of** [bɪˈkɔːz ʌv]
  因為……

5
宙斯之懲罰

費頓死於宙斯的雷霆之下。

p. 48

「請求宙斯，
若你不願饒恕我們，也請想想天庭。」
狄蜜特說：
「南極和北極已經出現濃煙，
這是支撐你天上宮殿的兩個極點，
如果極點被燒掉了，
你的宮殿就會墜毀，
擎天神阿特拉斯受不了這熱氣，
就快要無法將我舉起了。」
狄蜜特哀求著。
「倘若大地、海水和天庭消失了，
我們將回到遠古的渾沌狀態。」

p. 49

「啊，宙斯！
拯救這僅存的大地、海洋和天庭，
請不要再觀望了！
請立刻就行動，
盡快減輕我們的痛苦！」

- **spare** [sper] 饒恕
- **smoke** [smouk] 冒煙
- **support** [sə`pɔ:rt] 支持
- **destroy** [dɪs`trɔɪ]
  毀壞；破壞
- **Atlas** [`ætləs] 阿特拉斯
  （希神；以肩頂天的巨神）
- **barely** [`berli] 幾乎無法
- **continue to** 繼續去……
- **hold up** [hould ʌp]
  抬起
- **Chaos** [`keɪɑ:s] 渾沌
  （宇宙形成之前的狀態）

- **overcome with**
  以……戰勝；克服
- **throat** [θrout] 喉嚨
- **suffering** [`sʌfərɪŋ]
  苦難的經歷

28

說完，大地女神也熱得受不了，
她的喉嚨乾渴，說不出話來。

宙斯感受到大地上的痛苦，
也看到所有生物的苦難。
他召集所有神祉，
包括阿波羅在內，
宙斯在眾神前宣布，
他將停止這場毀滅。

- **includ** [ɪnˋkluːd]
  包含
- **would** [wʊd]
  （表示意願）想；要
- **destruction** [dɪˋstrʌkʃən]
  毀壞

---

p. 50

接著他走上指揮氣候的高台上，
當時天上沒有半點雲。

偉大的宙斯吆喝著，
雷聲從他口中發出，
閃電在他手中起舞。
他舉起手臂，目標瞄準費頓。
天空閃出一道白光，
接著傳來巨響，迴蕩在大地上，
馬車頓時粉碎，馬匹跑回原處，
費頓從天而落。

- **command** [kəˋmænd]
  命令；指揮
- **roar** [rɔː(r)] 吼叫
- **come from** 從……而來
- **raise** [reɪz] 舉起
- **aim** [eɪm] 瞄準
- **flash** [flæʃ] 閃光；閃爍
- **crash** [kræʃ] 爆烈聲
- **echo** [ˋekoʊ] 發出回聲
- **burst into** 爆裂成……

29

p. 51

阿波羅的神奇油脂，
無法保護費頓不被宙斯的閃電給擊傷。
費頓的身體燒了起來，
頭髮也著了火。
他冒著火煙的身體，
看起來就像一顆流星，
最後他落入了愛理達納河中。
現在，一切又歸於平靜，
大地一片黑暗。
〔圖〕費頓落河

- **protect** [prə`tekt] 保護
- **the river Eridanus**
  愛理達納河

p. 52

阿波羅失去馬車，
無法為大地帶來光與熱。
但就在馬車墜落地面之時，
火神已開始著手打造一輛新馬車。
他在隔天黎明女神奧羅拉醒來之前，
已經完工。

但阿波羅因喪子之慟，
不願駕駛新馬車。
他獨自坐在宮殿中悲痛欲絕。

- **as soon as**
  一……就……
- **start to**
  開始去……
- **Aurora** [ɔ`rɔːrə]
  奧羅拉（曙光女神）
- **awoke** [ə`wok] 使醒來
  （awake的過去式）
- **the loss of** 失去……

30

p. 53

因此，隔天大地仍舊沒有陽光，
人類和眾神再次求助於宙斯：
「我們需要陽光。」
「我們無法生活在寒冷與黑暗之中。」

宙斯和其他神祇前來說服阿波羅。
「你不能讓世界永遠黑暗。」宙斯說。
但是阿波羅對宙斯不諒解，
因為宙斯的雷霆，殺了費頓。

- **pass without**
  沒有……的經過了
  （時間）
- **live in** [lɪv ɪn] 住在……

p. 54

宙斯說，
「誠然，你失去愛子。
但是想想因他而死去的男女老少，
若我不有所行動，
整個大地將會消失在烈焰之中，
我別無選擇啊。」
最後，阿波羅接受宙斯的勸說，
戴上了他的冠冕。

- **whole** [houl]
  全部的；全體的
- **disappeare** [dɪsəˈpɪr]
  消失的
- **in flames** [ɪn fleɪms]
  在烈焰中
- **have no choice** 沒有選擇
  的；無可奈何的
- **agree with** [əˈgriː wɪθ]
  同意……
- **tie . . . to** 將……繫於

31

隔天，他將馬匹繫上新馬車，
接著黎明女神出現在東方天空。

- **appear** [ə`pɪr] 出現

---

 p. 55

阿波羅又開始他的天際旅程，
直到今日，始終如一。
從那天之後，
太陽再也不會運行得太高
或太低了。

- **once again** [wʌns ə`geɪn]
  再一次
- **across** [ə`krɔ:s] 橫越
- **even today** 即使今日
- **from that day on**
  從那天起

閱讀測驗

閱讀下列問題並選出最適當的答案。 ➜ 56-59 頁

1. 下列哪一項不是費頓在旅程中所曾做過的事？
   - (A) 他經過了印度。
   - (B) 他看見許多驚奇的事物。
   - (C) 他爬上一座山頭。
   - (D) 他在城市中探險。　　　　　　　　答案 (D)

2. 當費頓說他是太陽之子時，他的朋友是如何反應的？

   答案 Phaeton s friends laughed at him and want him to prove it.

   費頓的朋友們都笑他，並且要他加以證明。

3. 為什麼費頓一路上除了吃飯跟睡覺之外，都不肯停下腳步？
   - (A) 因為他想盡快和父親見面。
   - (B) 因為他對週遭事物都沒有興趣。
   - (C) 因為他很累。
   - (D) 因為他答應過他母親不停下來。　　答案 (A)

33

4. 阿波羅如何應允費頓，以證明自己就是他的父親？

答案 Apollo said that he would give Phaeton anything that Phaeton ask for.

阿波羅說會給費頓他想要的任何事物。

5. 阿波羅如何試著勸退費頓？（可複選）

(A) 他說即使是宙斯也無法駕馭馬車。

(B) 他說馬車對費頓來說火熱難耐。

(C) 他說費頓不是他兒子。

(D) 他說費頓會被大熊星座和小熊星座給殺了。

答案 (A), (B)

6. 阿波羅想嚇阻費頓，但費頓卻一點也不害怕。為什麼？

答案 Because Phaeton wanted to show the world that he was really Apollo s son.

因為費頓想要告訴全世界他的確就是太陽神之子。

7. 特殊的油脂對馬有什麼作用？

    (A) 它能使馬蹄更美麗。

    (B) 它使馬匹能飛行。

    (C) 它能使馬匹長得更大。

    (D) 它使馬匹能噴火。

                                 答案 (B)

8. 阿波羅教導費頓如何駕馭馬匹的最後指導是什麼？

   答案 Do not hit the horses to make them go faster.

    千萬不要鞭馬示意牠們快走。

9. 宙斯的雷霆閃電使得費頓怎麼了？

    (A) 它讓費頓的身體四分五裂了。

    (B) 它讓費頓的身體燒起來了。

    (C) 它讓費頓忘了所有的事情。

    (D) 它讓費頓變成一匹馬。

                                 答案 (B)

10. 這個故事告訴我們，為什麼衣索匹亞的人們都變黑黑的？

   答案 Because the Chariot flew over Ethiopia.

    因為費頓曾經駕馬車經過衣索比亞。

※閱讀下段文章，並討論以下的問題。

……為了要讓你證明，我會答應你的一切要求。
我就對著守誓河起誓，眾神都是在那裡立下重誓的。」
費頓立即回答，「我希望能夠駕駛你的馬車，父親。」
……你這一個願望太危險了。
……阿波羅想勸退費頓，但費頓不想改變心意。……

11. 阿波羅讓費頓駕馭馬車，費頓卻因而喪命。若你是阿波
    羅，你會怎麼做呢？

[參考答案]

I would have ridden in the chariot behind Phaeton to make
sure nothing bad happened, but I don t know if there was
enough room for two people.

我會和費頓一同坐在馬車上，以免發生任何災害，但我不知
道馬車座位是否坐得下兩個人。

……阿波羅想勸退費頓，但費頓不想改變心意。
……「我擔心這個禮物會奪走你的性命。」阿波羅說。
費頓聽著，卻絲毫不退縮。他想要向全世界證明，
他確是阿波羅之子。……

12. 費頓怎麼沒有想到用別的方法來證明阿波羅就是他的父
    親呢？如果你是費頓，你會怎麼向全世界證明你就是阿
    波羅之子？

[參考答案]

I would ask Apollo if I could live in his palace and learn from him.
Then everyone would know that I was Apollo s son.

我會請求阿波羅讓我住在他的宮殿中，並且向他學習，
這樣大家就都會知道我是太陽神之子了。

黃道十二宮

黃道十二宮 ➜ 64~68 頁

「黃道帶」（zodiac）這個字源自希臘文，意指「動物的環狀軌道」。黃道帶的起源為何？在本篇裡，你將可以看到說明星座來源的希臘神話故事：

太陽（the Sun）、地球（the Earth）、牡羊座（the Ram）、金牛座（the Bull）、雙子座（the Twins）、巨蟹座（the Crab）、獅子座（the Lion）、處女座（the Virgin）、天秤座（the Balance）、天蠍座（the Scorpion）、射手座（the Archer）、摩羯座（the Goat）、寶瓶座（the Water Bearer）、雙魚座（the Fishes）。

1. Aries（the Ram）牡羊座
2. Libra（the Balance）天秤座
3. Taurus（the Bull）金牛座
4. Scorpio（the Scorpion）天蠍座
5. Gemini（the Twins）雙子座
6. Sagittarius（the Archer）射手座
7. Cancer（the Crab）巨蟹座
8. Capricorn（the Goat）摩羯座
9. Leo（The Lion）獅子座
10. Aquarius（the Water Bearer）寶瓶座
11. Virgo（the Virgin）處女座
12. Pisces（the Fishes）雙魚座

牡羊座（the Ram） 3.21-4.20

牡羊座源自於金羊毛的故事。白羊安全營救福里瑟斯，福里瑟斯把金羊獻祭給宙斯作為回報，宙斯便將金羊形象化為天上星座。

金牛座（the Bull） 4.21-5.20

金牛座源自於歐羅巴和公牛的故事。宙斯化身為公牛，以便吸引歐羅巴，公牛載著歐羅巴跨海來到克里特島。宙斯將公牛的形象化為星座，以為紀念。

雙子座（the Twins） 5.21-6.21

雙子座源自於卡斯特與波樂克斯的故事。他們兩人為孿生兄弟，彼此相親相愛。為了紀念其兄弟情誼，宙斯將他們的形象化為星座。

巨蟹座（the Crab） 6.22-7.22

巨蟹座源自於赫丘力的十二項苦差役。希拉派遣巨蟹前去殺害赫丘力，但是赫丘力在打敗九頭蛇之前，一腳將巨蟹踩碎。爲了紀念巨蟹，希拉將其形象化爲星座。

獅子座（The Lion） 7.23-8.22

獅子座亦源自於赫丘力十二項苦差中。赫丘力的第一項苦差，是要殺死奈米亞山谷之獅。他徒手殺了獅子，爲了紀念這項偉大的事蹟，宙斯將奈米亞獅子的形象，置於星辰之中。

處女座（the Virgin） 8.23-9.22

處女座源自於潘朵拉的故事。處女指的是純潔與天眞女神阿絲蒂雅。潘朵拉好奇將禁盒打開，讓許多邪惡事物來到人間，眾神紛紛返回天庭。爲了紀念這種失落的純眞，便把阿絲蒂雅的形象置於群星中。

天秤座 （the Balance）　9.23-10.21

天秤是正義的秤子，由神聖正義女神蒂米絲隨身攜帶。天秤座落在處女座旁邊，因為阿絲蒂雅是蒂米絲之女。

天蠍座 （the Scorpion）　10.22-11.21

天蠍座源自於歐里昂。歐里昂和阿蒂蜜絲是一對狩獵夥伴，阿蒂蜜絲的哥哥阿波羅對此忌妒不已。他請求蓋亞殺了歐里昂。因此，蓋亞創造天蠍殺了偉大的歐里昂。為了紀念此事，宙斯將歐里昂和天蠍化成星座。這兩個星座從來不會同時出現。

射手座 （the Archer）　11.23-12.21

射手座代表卡隆。在希臘神話故事中，卡隆是許多英雄的朋友，例如亞吉力、赫丘力。赫丘力以毒箭誤傷了卡隆。卡隆是神，因此得以不死，但是卻必須忍受這無止盡的痛苦，所以卡隆央求宙斯殺了他。為了紀念卡隆，宙斯將他化為星座。

摩羯座 （the Goat）　12.22-1.19

魔羯代表哺育年幼宙斯的羊阿瑪爾夏。
據說宙斯為了感念此羊，將之化為星座。

寶瓶座 （the Water Bearer）　1.20-2.18

寶瓶座源自於鐸卡連的洪水。在這個故事中，宙
斯在人間降下豪雨，讓洪水沖走一切邪惡的生
物。只有鐸卡連和妻子皮雅是洪水的生還者。

雙魚座 （the Fishes）　2.19-3.20

雙魚座代表愛與美之女神阿芙柔黛蒂，
以及其子愛神愛羅斯。當時有個颱風，
兩人沿著優芙瑞特河步行。他們請求宙
斯援救，宙斯將兩人變成魚，讓他們安
然渡過風災。為了紀念此事，阿芙柔黛
蒂化身為星座中的大魚，愛羅斯則化為
小魚。

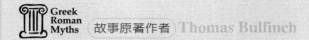

Without a knowledge of mythology much of the elegant literature of our own language cannot be understood and appreciated.

缺少了神話知識，就無法了解和透徹語言的文學之美。

—*Thomas Bulfinch*

Thomas Bulfinch（1796-1867），出生於美國麻薩諸塞州的Newton，隨後全家移居波士頓，父親為知名的建築師Charles Bulfinch。他在求學時期，曾就讀過一些優異的名校，並於1814年畢業於哈佛。

畢業後，執過教鞭，爾後從商，但經濟狀況一直未能穩定。1837年，在銀行擔任一般職員，以此為終身職業。後來開始進一步鑽研古典文學，成為業餘作家，一生未婚。

1855年，時值59歲，出版了奠立其作家地位的名作*The Age of Fables*，書中蒐集希臘羅馬神話，廣受歡迎。此書後來與日後出版的 *The Age of Chivalry*（1858）和 *Legends of Charlemagne*（1863），合集更名為 *Bulfinch's Mythology*。

本系列書系，即改編自 *The Age of Fable*。Bulfinch 著寫本書時，特地以成年大眾為對象，以將古典文學引介給一般大眾。*The Age of Fable* 堪稱十九世紀的羅馬神話故事的重要代表著作，其中有很多故事來源，來自Bulfinch自己對奧維德（Ovid）的《變形記》（*Metamorphoses*）的翻譯。

Bulfinch 的著作

1. Hebrew Lyrical History.
2. The Age of Fable: Or Stories of Gods and Heroes.
3. The Age of Chivalry.
4. The Boy Inventor: A Memoir of Matthew Edwards, Mathematical-Instrument Maker.
5. Legends of Charlemagne.
6. Poetry of the Age of Fable.
7. Shakespeare Adapted for Reading Classes.
8. Oregon and Eldorado.
9. Bulfinch's Mythology: Age of Fable, Age of Chivalry, Legends of Charlemagne.